# NORMAN BRIDWELL

# Clifford®

# GOES TO DOG SCHOOL

## SCHOLASTIC INC.

New York   Toronto   London   Auckland   Sydney

Mexico City   New Delhi   Hong Kong   Buenos Aires

To the children of

Carlisle Elementary School

ISBN 0-439-32788-1

Copyright © 2002 by Norman Bridwell.
All rights reserved. Published by Scholastic Inc.
SCHOLASTIC, CARTWHEEL BOOKS, and associated logos are trademarks
and/or registered trademarks of Scholastic Inc.
CLIFFORD, CLIFFORD THE BIG RED DOG, and associated logos are trademarks
and/or registered trademarks of Norman Bridwell.
Frisbee is a registered trademark of WHAM-O, INC.

Library of Congress Cataloging-in-Publication Data

Bridwell, Norman.
        Clifford goes to dog school / Norman Bridwell
                p.      cm.
        Summary: Auntie, who is a dog trainer, thinks Clifford needs to learn obedience, but to
Emily Elizabeth, the big dog is perfect already.
        ISBN 0-439-32788-1
        [1. Dogs — Fiction. 2. Dogs — Training — Fiction.]    I. Title.

        PZ7.B7633 Cji 2002
        [E] — dc21

                10                                          03 04 05 06
                        Printed in the U.S.A.
                    First printing, February 2002

I'm Emily Elizabeth. This is my dog, Clifford.
Clifford is a very smart dog. He can do tricks.

He can beg.

He can shake hands.

You really should see him play dead.

He's good at that.

I thought he was perfect, but my aunt didn't agree. She was a dog trainer. She said that no dog was perfect unless he had been to dog school, like her dog, Sandy.

Clifford was too big for regular dog school, so my aunt said she would train Clifford herself. First he had to learn to heel. He had to walk next to her on a leash.

That leash was a little too short.

Auntie got a longer leash for Clifford.

That leash was a little *too* long. Poor Auntie.

Auntie said we would come back to that lesson.

Next she told Clifford to sit. Clifford is very smart.

He sat.

Luckily, Clifford didn't sit down really hard.
The man wasn't hurt—just surprised.

Auntie said that Clifford was pretty good at sitting. Now he needed to learn how to stay. That meant not moving until he was told to move—no matter what happened.

She told him to sit and stay.

Auntie said she had some good books on dog training that I should see.

We went to her house a few blocks away.

She had so many good books about dogs! I love to read.

I guess I was so busy reading I forgot about Clifford.
He was still sitting and staying.

He knew he had to sit, no matter what happened.

Sandy moved, but Clifford stayed.

Even when a Frisbee flew by his nose, he stayed.

And Clifford loves to chase Frisbees.

Even when some dogs and cats played
near him, Clifford stayed. But it was hard.

Back at Auntie's house, I suddenly remembered Clifford. How could I have forgotten my dog?

I ran back to Clifford as fast as I could.

I wasn't very careful. I forgot to look both
ways when I crossed the street.

Clifford saved me!

I guess Clifford will never be the best-trained dog....

But to me, he'll always be the best dog in the world.